Belinda and the Bears Go Shopping

Belinda and the Bears Go Shopping

Kaye Umansky

Illustrated by
Chris Jevons

Orion
Children's Books

ORION CHILDREN'S BOOKS

First published in Great Britain in 2016
by Hodder and Stoughton

1 3 5 7 9 10 8 6 4 2

A CIP catalogue record for this book
is available from the British Library.

ISBN 978 1 4440 1354 2

Printed and bound in China

The paper and board used in this book are from well-managed forests
and other responsible sources.

Orion Children's Books
An imprint of Hachette Children's Group
Part of Hodder and Stoughton
Carmelite House
50 Victoria Embankment, London EC4Y 0DZ

An Hachette UK Company

www.hachette.co.uk
www.hachettechildrens.co.uk

For Ivy-Rose and Orlaith

Contents

Chapter One

There were two cottages in Honeybear Lane. One had a door painted green.
    Behind that door lived Belinda, with her mum, dad and a cat called Gertie.

Behind the blue door lived...
The Three Bears!

The Bears had come to live in Honeybear Lane when their house in the woods was knocked down to build a motorway. After that, and all the fuss with Goldilocks, they wanted a quiet life.

Belinda was sitting in the Bears' kitchen. Daddy Bear was in the garden. Baby Bear was on Mummy Bear's lap, rubbing his eyes and yawning.

"What's wrong with Baby?" asked Belinda.

"Tired," said Mummy Bear. "Every night, Daddy's snoring wakes him up. Then he wants a story or a glass of milk. Then I don't get any sleep. Every morning, he jumps on Daddy's tummy to wake him. So none of us are happy."

"Maybe he needs a room of his own," said Belinda. "Why don't you put him in the attic? Then you'd all sleep well."

"What?" said Mummy Bear.
"You mean – not sleep together?"

"Well, it must be squashed," said
Belinda. "Three beds in one room."

"It is," said Mummy Bear. "But Bears sleep together. We've always done it that way. He'd be scared on his own in the dark."

"You could give him a little lamp." Belinda turned to Baby, who was suddenly wide awake. "What do you think, Baby? Would you like a room of your own?"

"Yes!" shouted Baby Bear. "Want a room!"

He turned a cartwheel to show
how excited he was.

"We'll ask Daddy," said Mummy.
"But it's a very strange idea."

Chapter Two

Daddy Bear thought it was a
wonderful idea. He didn't like
having his tummy jumped on in
the morning.

The attic room had a sloping roof, bare floorboards and a tiny window that hadn't been cleaned for a long time.

"It's very gloomy," said Mummy Bear. "Look at all those cobwebs."

"It just needs a good clean," said Belinda, "It won't take long if we all help."

So that's what they did.

They all helped move Baby's bed.

"It looks very bare, doesn't it?"
said Mummy. "One little bed with
all that space around."

"Some furniture will make it cosy," said Belinda. "A bedside table and a chest of drawers for clothes. And a rug. We'll make a list, then go shopping. There's a junk shop in the village that sells all kinds of things."

The Bears looked at each other.

"We don't think we're ready for the village," said Daddy. "We're used to the woods, you see."

"The village will make a change," said Belinda.

"But we're bears," said Mummy. "People will stare."

"No they won't," said Belinda. "Everyone is friendly around here."

"They might run away," said Daddy.

"Of course they won't," said Belinda. "They'll love having bears in the village." Then she thought for a moment. "If it makes you feel better, you could go in disguise."

"Hooray!" shouted Baby. "Want to go shopping! Want to be Robin Hood!"

Chapter Three

Later that day, Belinda led the Bears to the village.

Daddy Bear was wearing a long coat, a floppy hat and a big pair of sunglasses.

Mummy Bear was wearing a cloak and a flowery hat with a veil.

Baby Bear skipped along in a Robin Hood hat.

Belinda couldn't help smiling. Nothing could hide the fact that they were Bears. But she didn't say so.

"Morning, Belinda!" called the postman. "Lovely day!"

"Morning, Mr Tucker," called Belinda.

Two ladies were coming out
of the butcher's shop. They both
jumped when they saw the Bears,
but managed to smile.

"Hello, Mrs Salt," called Belinda.
"Hello, Miss Pine."

"Morning, Belinda," said Mrs
Salt. "No school today?"

"It's a holiday," said Belinda.
"I'm taking my friends shopping."
"Well, that's nice," said Miss
Pine. "Er – enjoy yourselves."

Mr Todd the baker stood in his doorway. His mouth fell open when he saw who was coming.

"Morning, Mr Todd," called Belinda.

"Hello, Belinda," said Mr Todd. "Coming to buy some of my buns?"

"Not today, thank you. I'm helping my friends buy furniture."

"Well, good luck," said Mr Todd.

"I must say that everyone is very friendly," said Mummy Bear.

"You see?" said Belinda. "I told you."

Chapter Four

The junk shop was run by an old man with a beard and thick glasses. His name was Mr Musty. He looked up from behind the counter.

"Good morning, Belinda," said Mr Musty. "Can I help you?"

"I hope so," said Belinda. "We need to buy some things for Baby's bedroom. Here's the list."

The Bears were staring around at the wonderful things in the shop. Old clocks. Boxes full of battered books. A little red teapot. A china doll in a lacy dress. A bundle of walking sticks. An old trumpet. The place was a treasure trove.

Baby Bear picked up an old trumpet.

"Put it down, son," growled Daddy Bear. "Don't touch!"

"That's all right, let him have fun," said Mr Musty. "Now, I think I've got most of what you need. Follow me."

Mr Musty was right. He did have everything the Bears needed.

There was a tiny bedside table and a perfect little lamp to put on it.

There was a small chest of drawers, painted green.

There was a blue rug.

There was also a mirror to hang on the wall, and a picture of a fire engine that Baby Bear loved.

Mr Musty said he would deliver it all in his van and throw in the trumpet for Baby Bear, free of charge!

"I can't believe how nice everyone is," said Mummy as they walked back along Honeybear Lane. "Don't you agree, Daddy?"

"I do," said Daddy Bear. "Although, of course, they don't know we're bears."

Chapter Five

How different the attic room looked,
when everything was in place.

"It's so cosy," said Mummy Bear.

"What do you think, Baby?" asked Daddy Bear.

Baby thought it was just right. He couldn't wait to go to bed. He ran to put on his pyjamas.

"Good night, Baby," said
Mummy Bear, as she tucked him in.
"Night night," said Baby Bear.
He snuggled down in the lamp's
warm glow.

"Would you like a cup of tea, Belinda?" asked Mummy, when they went downstairs.

"No, thank you," said Belinda. "I should go home."

Just then, there was a pattering sound. Baby Bear came into the kitchen.

"What's the matter, son?" asked Daddy Bear. "Why aren't you in bed?"

"I'm scared," said Baby Bear. "I don't like it on my own."

"But you're a big boy now," said Mummy.

"And we're sleeping in the room below," said Daddy.

Baby Bear still looked sad.
Belinda wondered what she
could do to make him feel better.

Suddenly, she knew.
"I'm popping home to get
something," she said, "but I'll be
right back."

When Belinda returned, Baby
Bear was on Mummy Bear's lap
reading a book.

"Look who I've brought," said Belinda. And she held out her very own teddy bear.

"This is Teddy," said Belinda. "He always sleeps in my bed, but I told him about you, and he said he'd like to sleep in yours for a change."

Baby Bear hugged Teddy hard.

"He doesn't like being on his own," said Belinda. "You have to stay in bed to look after him. He needs a big bear like you to protect him. Do you want to show him your room?"

"Yes," said Baby Bear. He hurried up the stairs.

"Well," said Daddy Bear. "That worked wonders."

"Thank you, Belinda," said Mummy Bear.

"You're welcome," said Belinda. "I hope you get a good night's sleep."

Chapter Six

That night, Belinda lay in her own bed. She missed Teddy, but Baby Bear needed him more.

"Did you have a good day?" asked her dad, when he came for his goodnight kiss.

"Yes," said Belinda. "I went shopping with the Bears."

"Is that so?" asked her dad. "What did you buy?"

"Furniture for Baby Bear's new room. It looks lovely now."

"What did they think of the village?" said her dad.

"They liked it. They were scared at first. They would only come in disguise. But everyone knew they were bears anyway." Belinda giggled.

"You're a big help to those Bears," said her dad, as he turned out the light.

"I know," said Belinda happily. "I really don't know what they'd do without me."